For May and Conan. —AH
For Kylie. —NS

LETTERS

First published in the United States in 2021 by Sourcebooks
Text © 2020, 2021 by Alice Hemming
Illustrations © 2020, 2021 by Nicola Slater
Sourcebooks and the colophon are registered trademarks of Sourcebooks.
All rights reserved.

The sketches and full color art were created in Photoshop, with the occasional scanned paint or graphite texture added here and there.

Published by Sourcebooks Jabberwocky, an imprint of Sourcebooks Kids
P.O. Box 4410, Naperville, Illinois 60567-4410
(630) 961-3900
sourcebookskids.com

Originally published in 2020 in the UK by Scholastic Children's Books, a division of Scholastic Ltd.

Library of Congress Cataloging-in-Publication Data is on file with the publisher.

Source of Production: C&C Offset Printing
Date of Production: March 2023
Run Number: 5031387

Printed and bound in China.
CC 10 9 8 7

FSC
MIX
Paper | Supporting responsible forestry
FSC® C008047
www.fsc.org

the LEAF THIEF

ALICE HEMMING

NICOLA SLATER

sourcebooks
jabberwocky

"What a **wonderful** time of year!
I am snug in my nest with a belly full of hazelnuts
and the sun is shining through my leafy canopy.
Such lovely colors:

red, gold, orange...

red, gold, orange...

red, gold...

Wait a MINUTE!

One of my leaves is..."

"Your... leaf?"

"Yes. One of my leaves is MISSING. My leaf looked a lot like that one. The one Mouse has."

"That is not your leaf, Squirrel."

"But how can you be sure? Mouse? Mouse! Did you steal my leaf?"

"No.
This is my
boat."

"See, Squirrel?
It is perfectly normal to lose
a leaf or two at this time of
year... OK?"

"OK, thanks, Bird.
See you tomorrow."

The following morning...

This is a
DISASTER!

Bird?

BIRD!

WHERE ARE
YOU, BIRD?

"I'm here,
Squirrel."

"WAIT A MINUTE...

are YOU the LEAF THIEF?"

"No, Squirrel.
I am not the Leaf Thief.
I will SHOW you the
Leaf Thief."

"Where are they?
Because I've got a few things
I'd like to say to them!"

"Look around you.
The Leaf Thief is everywhere.

It shakes the trees...

and rustles the leaves...

It even takes your hat!

Do you see the Leaf Thief, Squirrel?"

"The only thief is the **WIND**!
This happens every year in the autumn. Every year!
The leaves change colors and the wind blows them away.
They'll grow back again in the spring.
Now, I'm going home. Please don't disturb me again."

"It was just the wind.
The leaves change colors and the wind blows them away.
Of course! No Leaf Thief at all. Silly me.
I'm going to sleep well tonight!"

The Real Leaf Thief

As squirrel learned, nobody is really stealing the leaves from the trees.

Bird says,
"The only thief is the WIND."

But there is more to it than that. The wind can only blow the leaves away when the trees have started to shed their leaves. This happens in the autumn when the temperature drops, marking the change from summer to winter.

Trees look very pretty in the autumn.

Before the leaves fall, they turn from green to all sorts of different colors.

"Red, gold, orange..."

When they turn brown, the leaves are ready to fall from the tree.